P9-BYJ-459

Just Right

BY LILIAN MOORE

ILLUSTRATIONS BY *Aldren A. Watson*

Parents' Magazine Press

NEW YORK § 1968

Printed in the United States of America
Library of Congress Catalog Card Number: 68-11658

For Leone—
who cares about ponds and meadows

Old Mr. West had a farm.

There was a pond on this farm, and in the pond there were fish and frogs and turtles.

There were woods on the farm, and in the woodland
lived birds and small animals and the white-tailed deer.
There was a meadow, too, where all day long
the grasshoppers cricked and the crickets chirped.
Farmer West loved the farm.
But he was getting old.

One day he said to his wife, “The time has come
to sell the farm. It is too big
for me now. There is too much work to do.”
His wife looked at him, surprised.
“Sell the farm? But you were a boy here!”
“I know,” said Farmer West.

"And our boy, Robbie," said his wife.

"He grew up here, too."

"I know," said Farmer West. "But Robbie is a man now,

and he has gone away to the city to live.

His boy, Tommy, will grow up there.

I must sell the farm."

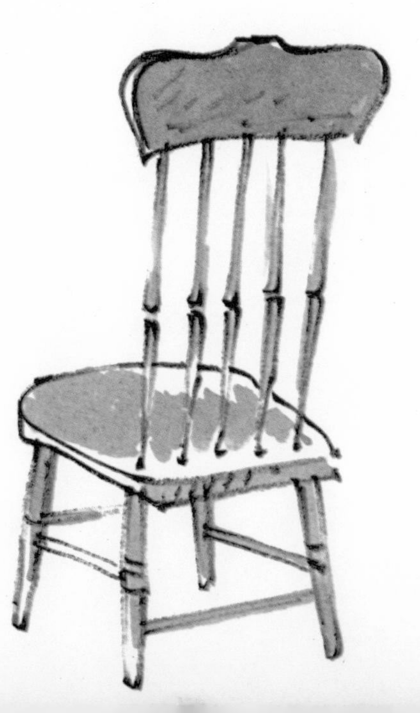

That day Farmer West looked around for a sturdy
piece of wood. In the barn he found a good piece of oak
that would stand up to wind and weather. Then he made a sign
that said FOR SALE, and when it was finished
he walked out to the road and put it up.

0615

WEST

One day a car stopped at the farmhouse.

The man in the car said to Farmer West,

"I want to buy a farm. I see this one is for sale.

May I look around?"

Farmer West showed him the farm.

The man liked everything he saw.

He liked the big red barns and the cozy white farmhouse.

He liked the broad fields and the woods.

But when they came to the pond he stopped.

The pond was like a looking glass showing upside-down trees and an upside-down sky in an upside-down world. A duck came swimming along, making an upside-down duck in the pond mirror.

"This farm is just right," said the man. "I like everything but this pond. I'll have to dry it out."

"Dry out the pond!" said Farmer West.

"Why, all kinds of things live there. All kinds of pond plants and pond creatures."

He kneeled down and cupped his hands

and let the cool pond water trickle through his fingers.

“This water comes running down from the brooks,” he said,

“and it soaks deep into the soil. Keeps the land

from getting thirsty.”

“But I want more land for planting,” said the man,

“so I’ll have to dry out the pond.”

“No,” said Farmer West. “I will not sell my farm to you.”

WEST

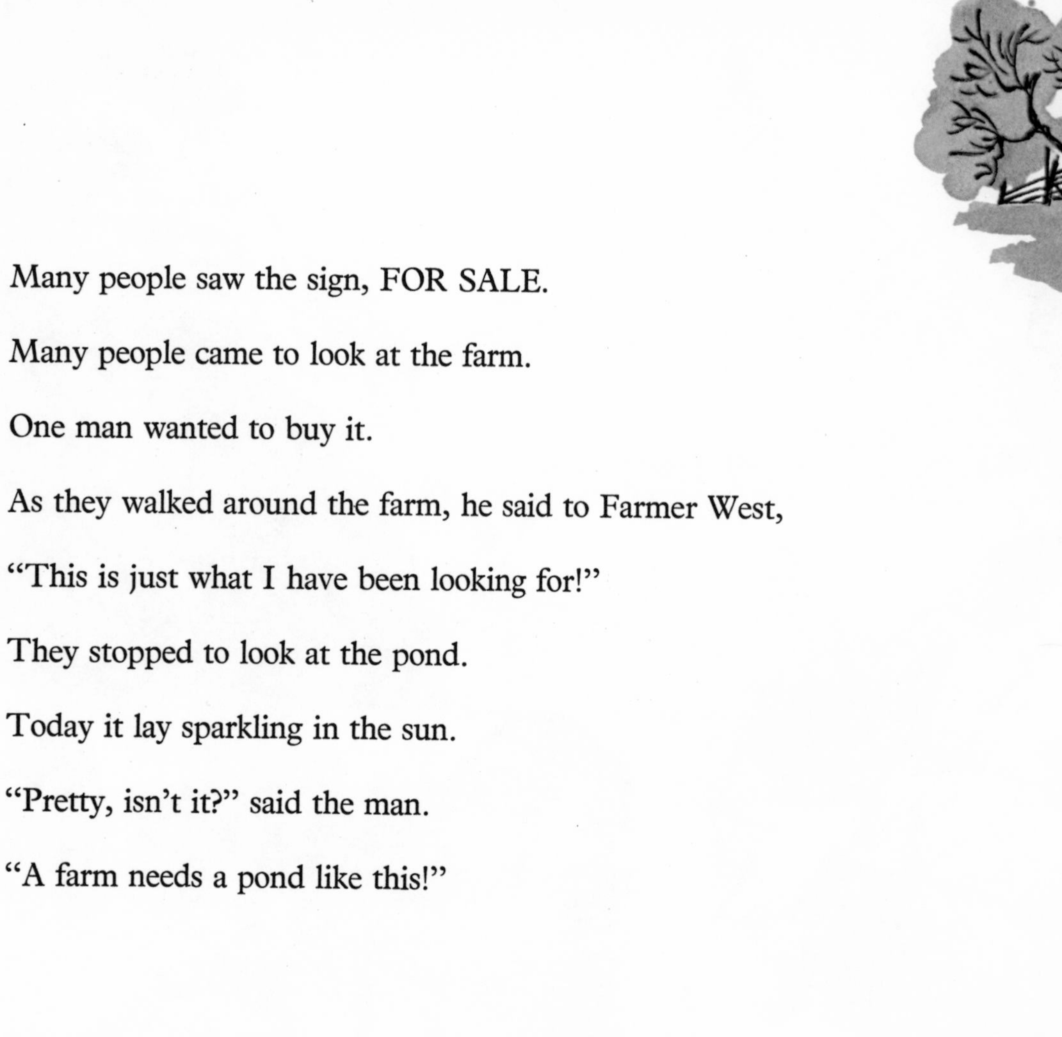

Many people saw the sign, FOR SALE.

Many people came to look at the farm.

One man wanted to buy it.

As they walked around the farm, he said to Farmer West,

“This is just what I have been looking for!”

They stopped to look at the pond.

Today it lay sparkling in the sun.

“Pretty, isn’t it?” said the man.

“A farm needs a pond like this!”

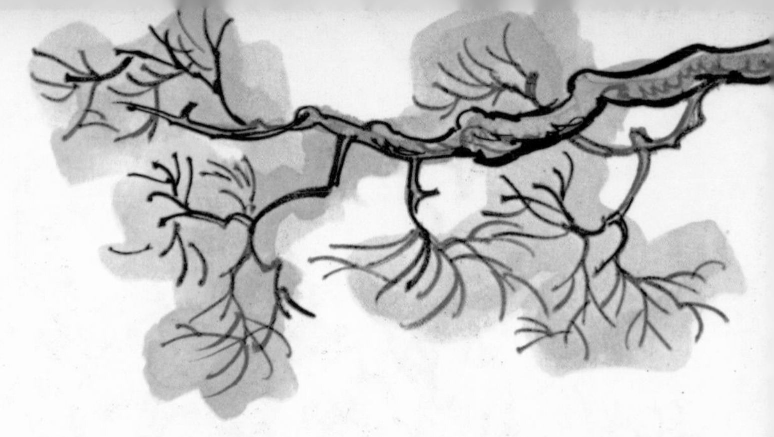

Farmer West smiled to himself

and they started back to the farmhouse.

The path took them past the woods.

The man stopped at the woods and looked around.

The woodland air was cool and wet and leafy,

and the trees were noisy with bird songs.

"This is a fine lot of trees," said the man.

"Yes," said Farmer West.

He touched the bark of a tall oak.

"Some of these trees are older than I am."

"They ought to bring a lot of money," said the man.

"I'd like to cut them down and sell them."

"Cut down these trees?" said Farmer West.

"No. I will not sell my farm to you."

One day a man and his wife saw the sign, FOR SALE.

They stopped, too, and wanted to see the farm.

They walked all around the farm with Farmer West.

And they said to each other again and again,

"Why this is just right—just what we want!"

They looked at the pond and told each other how much they liked it. "It is so cool here!" said the wife. They stopped in the woods and told each other how happy it made them. "It is so quiet here!" said the man.

“We like everything here,” the man told Farmer West,

“except that big old meadow.

I’d want to take out all that grass.

It would make a good field for corn.”

“Take out the meadow grass!” said Farmer West.

And he did not sell the farm to the man and his wife.

Farmer West did not go back to the farmhouse.

He sat in the meadow on a tree stump, thinking.

He heard the clear whistle of the meadow lark,

and he thought about that. Here in a secret clump of grass,

the mother meadow lark had her nest. But no one’s ever

going to find it, thought Farmer West.

She never flies up from the nest or down to it.

Always walks to it through the grass.

It began to rain, and Farmer West thought about that.

How gently the rain fell on the meadow grass

and how lightly it fell to earth!

Soon the rain would soak into the soil

and down into the grass roots.

Some of it would run into the tunnels

of the meadow mice

and be held there for a time. After a while

some of the rainwater would find its way

into the well on the farm.

Some of it would trickle into the stream and pond.

Farmer West thought about the pond

and the pond creatures, too.

He thought about the woods and the old trees.

But then he thought how big the farm was

and how much work there was to be done.

When he got back to the farmhouse, he said to his wife,

"I must get rid of the farm very soon.

I'm going to sell it to the

next one who wants it—*no matter what!*

And I must tell Robbie so."

Farmer West sat down and wrote a letter

to his son in the city.

Then he walked slowly out to the road to mail it.

The mailbox stood beside the sign that said FOR SALE.

Farmer West looked at the sign.

Then he dropped the letter into the box.

A few days later a car drove up the road,

and stopped at the farm.

Farmer West and his wife were sitting

in the kitchen when they heard it.

They looked at each other.

"*No matter what!*" said Farmer West.

Suddenly a boy came running up to the farmhouse yelling,

"Grandpa! Grandma! We're here! We're here!"

"Why—it's Tommy!" cried Farmer West.

"Mother, look! It's Tommy!"

Right behind Tommy came Robbie and his wife.

"Yes, we're here!" said Robbie.

How much there was to talk about!

It seemed they would never be done.

Then Robbie said, "We want to come back here to live.

I want Tommy to grow up the way I did

—to fish in the pond and play in the meadow . . ."

"And I want to climb all the trees!" cried Tommy.

That day Farmer West walked out to the road and took down the sign that said FOR SALE.

When his wife saw the sign she said gaily, "I'll be happy to throw it into the stove."

Farmer West turned the sign round in his hand.

Then he shook his head.

"No," he said. "It's a good piece of wood, and it will be just right."

"Just right for what?" asked Tommy.

Farmer West smiled.

"Just right for you and me to make a birdhouse," he said.

LILIAN MOORE is the author of many books for young children including *I Feel the Same Way*, *Little Raccoon and the Outside World*, and *Once Upon a Season*. As a member of the Bureau of Educational Research of the New York City Board of Education, she worked for many years as a reading specialist. Mrs. Moore has contributed countless beginning-reader stories to *Humpty Dumpty's Magazine* and other publications for children. Last year *The Magic Spectacles*, a collection of her easy-to-read stories, was published by Parents' Magazine Press.

ALDREN A. WATSON has illustrated over 160 books for children, many of these written by his wife, Nancy Dingman Watson, including *Katie's Chickens*, *Sugar on Snow*, and *Annie's Spending Spree*. He is both the author and illustrator of *My Garden Grows* and *The Village Blacksmith*. The Watsons live in Putney, Vermont with their eight children. The oldest, Wendy, is already making a name for herself in children's book illustration. Mr. Watson studied at Yale University and the Art Students League in New York.